THE ALIEN'S MATE

GRACE KENSINGTON

1

———

The air smelled like smoke and fire again, but this time as Ivy leaned against the stone wall at the back of the settlement, the smell didn't make her stomach turn. She remembered that first night that she had breathed in the acrid, burning smell of the flames that licked the sky. It was painful then, a harsh reminder of the funeral that was happening in the settlement below. That was the night that they had honored the dead that the settlement had lost to the Covra. She had run from the flames that night, wanted to get away from the mourning that made the air as thick as the smoke. That was the night that she had met Maxim.

The smell of the flames was celebratory now, but she had still run from them. The people in the settlement below lit the fires to burn the final reminders of the Covra and to celebrate the release of the Mikana from their captivity in the meeting hall. A mix of Denynso, Mikana, and humans swarmed the main street, dancing, singing, and feasting. Ivy stood on the hill that rose at the back of the settlement, her back against the stone wall. She had run from the flames, but not because she wanted to escape them. Not because they frightened and sickened her the way that the funeral fires had, but because she craved the darkness and privacy of that distant wall. Like the night of the fires, Maxim stood in front of her.

She was still enraptured by his intense beauty. Even though he was completely familiar now, known to her heart, mind, and body unlike any other man had ever been, she still found herself stopping sometimes just to look at him. His incredible beauty was by merit of being a part of the Mikana tribe. Every member of his kind had the ethereal appeal, and it was that appeal that made it even more shocking to find out that they were the predecessors of the grisly, slimy Klimnu. She had seen only part of Maxim's skin dissolving away as a reaction to the flowers that he had touched the first time that they had made love, and even that small amount of change had been truly terrifying. She couldn't even imagine what it was like to see the full Klimnu, creatures who had transformed under the power of the flowers and their own greed and hatred. The other women had tried to describe the creatures to her, pulling on their own horrifying memories of their encounters with them, but Ivy didn't think that those descriptions ever could have done justice for what those gruesome beings truly were.

In that moment, however, none of that mattered. She didn't care what Maxim had the potential to become. She cared only what he was, and that was the man who she loved with a depth that was almost unimaginable even as she was feeling it, the partner who she had chosen and who she was willing to face fear, danger, and hardship for by staying on Uoria rather than going home. Maxim was every-thing to her, and even though she ached to return home to

Earth and put the horrors that she had experienced on Uoria behind her, she knew that as long as he was here and as long as he was still searching for the answers to all of the questions that had come up once the Denynso arrived at the settlement, she would be by his side.

Ivy reached out for Maxim and took him into her arms. His body pressed against hers, pushing her back more firmly against the wall so that he enveloped her as his mouth took over hers. He kissed her languidly, his hands grazing down the sides of her ribs and into the dip of her waist. She could feel the rhythm of his heartbeat against her chest where the rhythm of her own responded, drumming against her as if reaching through their bodies toward one another. She wanted to stay right in that moment forever, to not have to let him go or even relinquish the indulgent taste of his tongue in her mouth, but she knew that she had to. They were waiting for him down in the settlement. There was a banquet happening and he was expected to be a part of it alongside his brother and the others of his kingdom.

She took her mouth slowly and reluctantly from his and touched the tip of his nose with hers.

"We should go back," she said softly.

Maxim gave a deep sigh and nuzzled his body closer against hers.

"I know," he whispered back. "I would rather just stay up here with you, though. Maybe take a little walk outside of the settlement."

He leaned around to nibble at her ear with his suggestion and she gave a soft laugh.

"I don't think that we need any more skin dissolving emergencies," she said.

"I'm sure that we could avoid the flowers this time."

"They are throwing a banquet down there in honor of

your people. Don't you think that you should be down there?"

He tilted his head as though he were thinking through his options.

"No," he said with a smile. "I would still rather be up here with you."

"What about your brother?" she asked, laughing as Maxim tucked his head to kiss along the side of her neck.

"He can find his own woman. I've never liked sharing and I'm not going to start now."

He ran the tip of his tongue in the curve between her neck and her shoulder and Ivy shivered slightly. She wanted to take that walk with him. She wanted to push their way through the old, forgotten gate as they had that night several days after the funeral fires, and disappear into the darkness of the fields and hills beyond the settlement. She wanted to feel his body against her skin and welcome him into her body in the way that made her feel safe, comfortable, and alive. She knew, though, that it was his responsibility to go back to the celebration. He had been instrumental in ensuring that the rest of the Mikana were released from the meeting hall where Pyra had ordered that they be put into what he called quarantine, but what Ivy knew was simply imprisonment. The leader of the Denynso warriors had been overcome with anger and hatred that day, and had let his power over the other warriors and the intimidation of the humans force them to enclose all of the Mikana in half of the main room of the meeting hall. If it hadn't been for Maxim's courage and determination, they would likely have all died there.

Ivy smiled as she thought of the wall that Loralia had made in the middle of the meeting hall room. It had truly been a reflection of the ceiling, put in place to prevent the captive Mikana from leaving that portion of the building. Though at the time Ivy couldn't understand the level of cruelty and disregard for life that had influenced the strange and beautiful creature to make that wall, she soon learned that it was how Loralia ensured that Ivy would be able to free Maxim. By suggesting to her that she simply not believe that the wall was there, she would be able to get him out so that together they could figure out what they were to do next. What she had learned, however, was that she didn't need to believe that the wall wasn't there, but that Maxim was. It had gotten him out of the room the night that he had been put into captivity, and just the night before it had made the entire wall disappear, leaving the room open again and removing the tangible reminder of Pyra's misguided decision.

"Come on," she said, playfully pushing on his shoulders to move his exploring mouth away from her even though the last thing she wanted was to lose the feeling of those lips and that skilled tongue on her skin. "There's a lot to be done."

Maxim stepped back from her and nodded.

"I know." He paused and reached up to brush a strand of her thick blond hair away from her face. "I love you."

Ivy felt the same shiver through her body that she always did when he said those words. They were wonderful and precious and inextricably hers. Each time that she heard them it was a reminder that he was real, the he felt the same passion and devotion for her that she did for him.

"I love you, too," she said.

Ivy lifted her lips up to accept the kiss that Maxim touched to them before he took her hand and started leading her down the hill back toward the revelry in the settlement. As they walked down past the meeting hall she noticed a dark shape lingering close to one of the walls, staying in the shadows rather than stepping out into the light created by the fire.

"Hello?" she called to the shape.

It stepped forward and she could see that it was Vax, the warrior who had followed so closely behind Pyra during his brief but terrifying reign over the settlement, and who had stepped in to ensure that Pyra's commands were upheld even as they left the settlement to return to the Denynso compound for Creia's guidance. Ivy fought the urge to step back away from the huge man. As much as she didn't want to admit it, she feared this warrior, possibly even more than she had ever feared Pyra. Even though the lead warrior had been vicious and single-minded in his determination to destroy the Mikana because of their link to the Klimnu, he had recanted. He had knelt before Creia and asked for his forgiveness for the choices that he had made and for losing the faith and the trust of his people. Though Ivy hadn't yet been able to bring herself to fully forgive him, she at least knew that he had recognized the wrong that he had done and wanted to change his ways.

Vax, however, had made no such move. Even after they told him that his leader had changed his mind and had gone back on his assertions that the Mikana should be killed, Vax would not back down. He had had no choice but to follow the proclamation from Creia that officially freed all of the captive Mikana. Even as he did it, however, he had shown nothing but contempt and fury. Ivy could still see in Vax's eyes the darkness and empty, sullen stare that told her that he had not let go of the fury that he had felt, or the desire for vengeance that he had thought he passionately shared with Pyra. In holding onto these feelings and now knowing that he was no longer supported and validated by his adored leader, Vax became unpredictable, and that was unnerving for Ivy.

Giving into the intimidation and stepping back away from Vax, however, would have given the warrior too much power and only reinforced his sense of superiority and control. She wouldn't give him that.

"Why did you have to come back?" Vax asked in a low, gravelly voice.

"I came back for my brother and the rest of my kind," Maxim said, tightening his grip on Ivy's hand slightly.

"Not you," Vax said. He turned to Ivy and she felt the animosity radiating off of the warrior. "You," he said. "Why did you have to come back?"

"I am here to be with Maxim," Ivy answered.

Vax gave a mirthless laugh and stepped toward them. Ivy still refused to back up.

"Why?"

"I love him."

"How could you do that?" Vax asked. "He isn't one of us."

"I'm not one of you," Ivy replied defensively.

"You came to the Denynso compound. You made the agreement to follow our ways."

"I came to the Denynso compound to learn your ways and find out more about your kind. I made no agreement to be anything like you, or to change in any way."

"The other human women who came here joined the clan."

"The other human women found their mates among the Denynso. That has nothing to do with me. Pyra had no power over me and you don't either. I have no obligation to the Denynso."

"Creia will feel differently about that," Vax said. "There are laws and regulations."

"Don't start that again, Vax. That's been done. I have followed the laws and the regulations. Creia released me from my guard. Pyra thought that he was going to agree with him about the Mikana and order them be destroyed, but he didn't. He is ready to welcome them into the compound and build alliances again. It's over. It's time to let it go."

"It will never be over."

2

———

Maxim's eyes squared on Vax. The huge warrior's words were cold and threatening, but Maxim wouldn't let himself react. It was what Vax wanted. He could see in the Denynso's eyes that he was hoping that Maxim would lose control and attack him, proving that he and his kind really were as vicious and uncontrollable as Pyra and Vax had said they were from the beginning. Maxim refused to give him that satisfaction and to feed into the hatred that drove Vax into the shadows and made him seethe with an anger that had nowhere to go.

Maxim held Ivy's hand tighter and pulled her back away from Vax. Without saying anything, he turned and led her back onto the main street and toward the celebration that was still going toward the center of the settlement. The warrior's provocation continued to burn in the back of his mind as they approached, but he pushed it away when he saw his brother standing among others of their clan and some of the humans, a large cup in one and a chunk of bread in the other. Kyven took a deep sip from the cup and then tore off a piece of the bread with his teeth. Maxim didn't want to think about how hungry and thirsty his younger brother was. He knew that some of the human women had tried to bring them food and water, but he would be very surprised if he found out that the Denynso guards actually permitted them to go to the men more than a few times since they had left.

Kyven looked up and caught sight of Maxim. Maxim saw a smile break across his face. A moment later his brother rushed toward him and Maxim let go of Ivy to gather Kyven into his arms. He had been free only one day and Maxim was still thrilled every time that he saw him able to move around as he pleased, alive and safe. There was still guilt deep in his chest for leaving with Ivy, even though he knew that it was only his leaving that made it possible for them to rescue the Mikana. When his father died he had promised his mother that he would take care of Kyven and make sure that he stayed safe. He felt like leaving him in that room rather than trying to get him out along with him was going against his promise to his mother and a dishonor to the memory of their father. As Kyven grinned and took a deep swig from the stein in his hand, however, Maxim felt a sense of relief. Everything worked out exactly as he would have hoped it would and he knew that his brother was safe.

"Have you had anything to eat?" Kyven asked, looking between Ivy and Kyven.

Maxim realized that in all of the chaos he hadn't actually introduced the two of them.

"Kyven, this is Ivy. Ivy, this is my younger brother Kyven."

"It's wonderful to meet you, Kyven," Ivy said.

"It's great to meet you, Ivy," Kyven said, giving Maxim a knowing look.

Maxim wrapped his arm around Ivy's waist and gave her a squeeze, leaning forward to press a kiss to her temple.

"Have you had anything to eat?" Kyven asked again.

Maxim laughed.

"You never change, do you?" he asked. "Always thinking about food."

As soon as he said it, Maxim regretted it. He didn't want to think about his brother being hungry in the meeting hall, and more than anything wanted to know that he was happy and comfortable. He gave him the biggest smile that he could manage, trying to press forward before Kyven could notice what he had asked and comment on it.

"What is there to eat?" he asked.

Kyven smiled again and gestured for them to follow him. They wove through the crowds filling the street, moving closer to the massive fire they had built near the wall created by Loralia to block the Covra when the warriors were still fighting them before the others from the compound arrived to help. The wall stood in the middle of the street, a reminder of everything that they had gone through and the efforts made to save the humans at the settlement from the fearsome creatures.

When Maxim had first arrived at the settlement with the rest of his kind and heard about the struggles that the Denysno had had with the Covra, Maxim had wished that he had been a part of the battles, had been able to witness the incredible tactics of the Denynso warriors. Now, though, he was glad that he hadn't been there. He didn't know then that it wasn't actually the Denynso warriors but a woman, the last of her species, who had been able to utilize her incredible abilities from the compound to create the towering wall of spikes that destroyed the advancing Covra. Had he known, Loralia creating the wall that had held them within the room of the meeting hall would have had a deeper, more painful impact. Standing beside them as they created a wall to defeat a hated enemy only to watch as the same people who he had fought alongside imprisoned them in the same cruel way.

Several people seemed to have dragged tables out of their homes and arranged them near the fire, piling them with food and full steins. The celebration wasn't like the banquets held in the kingdom, but there was something exuberant and informal about it that made Maxim feel energized and excited. He grabbed a stein and took a long swallow of the thick, spicy drink inside. He took a moment to look around at the people celebrating in the street. He noticed a few people standing at the outskirts of the celebration, seeming disconnected and distanced from the rest of the people in a way that was obvious and uncomfortable. Though there were only a small number of them, the expressions of ill feelings on their faces seemed to link them even across the space between them.

"I see that not everyone is as happy as they should be," Ivy said beside him and Maxim looked down at her.

He kissed the top of her head and gave her waist another squeeze.

"It will pass. Soon they will learn that we are moving forward and they have little choice but to come along with us," he said, hoping that he could convince himself of the same thing. "The future will be different for everyone on this planet and anyone who ever visits it. But we will face that when it comes tomorrow. Tonight, we celebrate."

BY THE TIME Maxim awoke early the next morning, the celebration felt like a distant memory. Even the sweetness of Ivy's naked body pressed against his in the predawn light wasn't enough to take the thoughts of his torturous dreams out of his mind. In those dreams he saw the face of his father, the details hazy and indistinct over time, and heard the sobs of his mother in the days, weeks, and months after they found out about his death. He saw the anger in Pyra's eyes, and the cold disconnection in Ciyrs's expression when the healer pressed his fingers into the dissolving place on Maxim's skin, revealing once and for all that he was reacting to the flowers as the Klimnu had. The dreams were brutal, painful flashes of shattered memories interspersed with thoughts of what could have been and what could still be if they didn't find out more about the Order and what had happened leading up to his father's death.

He knew that they couldn't wait any longer. He had come back to the settlement not just to free Kyven and make sure that the rest of his kind were safely freed. He had come back to dedicate himself to resolving the questions that lingered over him and the shadowy secrets that he felt some people would rather leave in the shadows.

Maxim climbed out of bed carefully, trying not to disturb Ivy. He dressed and turned to take a moment just to look at her. The sun was just started to creep up the horizon, allowing a small amount of blue light into the room. It was just enough to illuminate her where she lay on her belly on the bed, her hair spread around her and the blanket flung down low over her body so that he could see the swells of her breasts pressing to the bed and the soft curve of her hips just revealed by the edge of the cover. Her full lips, still slightly swollen and darkened by his kiss, were parted as she breathed and he reached to run his fingertips along them.

Ivy's eyes opened at his touch and she smiled at him sleepily before realizing that he was fully dressed and getting a confused, concerned look on her pretty face.

"I'm sorry, my love," he whispered to her. "I didn't mean to wake you. Go on back to sleep."

"What are you doing?" Ivy asked. "Where are you going?"

"I'm just going to talk with Kyven," Maxim told her, running his hand down her back tenderly. "It's alright. Sleep."

Ivy sat up and Maxim's eyes fell to her breasts. His stomach clenched, but he forced himself to concentrate on what needed to be done.

"I'm going with you," Ivy said insistently. "I agreed to be a part of this, and that means being a part of all of it. You can't just decide to leave me out of things."

"I wasn't leaving you out," Maxim told her. "I'm just going to talk to him and find out if he knows anything else about our father or the Order that he hasn't told me."

"I'm coming with you."

Maxim knew that he had little chances of convincing his partner of anything that she didn't want, so he waited as she climbed out of bed and padded around the room dressing. Even with the heaviness that had settled back over him with the taunting of his dreams, Maxim felt an overwhelming sense of gratefulness for her. He knew that no matter what he was going to face in the journey that lay ahead of him, she would be what was going to make it worth it, and what was going to give him the strength to carry it through.

3

***

Eden trembled slightly as she approached the shuttle, with Lysander tucked against her chest. She could feel Pyra's hand rested protectively against her lower back and felt comforted by its presence, but the gleaming shuttle positioned in the circular platform still sent a strange shiver of nervousness through her. It had been less than a year since she had first arrived on Uoria, but it felt like it had been a lifetime. She could no longer imagine living anywhere but in the Denynso compound with Pyra and the rest of the clan, and she felt oddly uncomfortable with the thought of getting back on the shuttle and traveling days away from the home that she had adopted as hers.

She had argued so passionately against Pyra to convince him that her and their son traveling to Earth with the rest of them was what was right for them, but even that conviction didn't change the anxiety that was starting to build in her stomach. At once she knew what was waiting for her on Earth and had no idea what might have changed. She knew that back at the research center Ryan was still working on his potentially less than ethical projects, and she knew that even though she had never returned and had made no effort to contact him, he hadn't done anything to make sure that she had even survived the trip to the planet, much less if she was still doing well there.

This didn't really surprise her. She had already resigned herself to the knowledge that Ryan hadn't sent her to the planet because he believed in her scientific abilities or really thought that she was going to be successful with the mission that he had created for her. Instead, he had sent her to the Denynso with the mission of collecting some of their blood in hopes that she would be caught by the warriors. Attempting to gather some of the highly desirable, incredible powerful blood from the fearsome Denysno warriors was the single most serious crime that a visitor to the Denynso compound on Uoria could commit. This single offense could result in imprisonment, exile, and even death. That was what Ryan was counting on, Eden had come to realize. She had rejected his advances and threatened to tell his superiors how he treated her and how much of the work that he presented as his own was actually hers. By sending her on this mission he was hoping that she would make a mistake and get caught, never having the chance to return to Earth and make good on her threats.

She wondered what he had been doing in the time that she had been gone. The impression that he had given her was that most of the research that he had been doing when she left had been hinging on her coming back with the Denynso warrior blood. He convinced her that it was that blood that would allow him to complete the research projects that they had started and complete some experiments that could completely change the face of weaponry. Eden hadn't really understood what he meant by that then, but now that she knew the Denynso warriors, the thought of someone utilizing their blood to craft weapons was truly terrifying. These were massive, fearsome warriors prone to aggressive, violent reactions and capable of relentless battle. Their blood held the source of this power, and if Ryan got hold of it the results could be disastrous.

"What are you thinking about?" Pyra asked softly as they gathered at the base of the platform to await boarding.

Eden's eyes were trained on the second shuttle beside the first and she shook her head slightly.

"Just Ryan."

"Why are you thinking about him?" he asked.

She could hear the defensiveness in his voice and regretted saying anything. Her mate was incredibly protective of her and their son and he hated to hear anything about the man who made her life so difficult when she was on Earth and then sent her to what he figured would either be her certain death or his ticket to fame and wealth.

"He sent me to Uoria because he wanted me to try to steal blood from one of the Denynso warriors," she said.

"I know," Pyra responded. "We've already talked about this. But you made the very wise decision to not go through with that and to stay with me instead," he said with a smile.

"But now I'm heading right back to Earth with a whole group of warriors."

The smile faded from Pyra's face and his hand slid around her waist to hold her more closely.

"He wouldn't try anything," Pyra said. "He might have thought it was a good idea to go after our blood when he wasn't anywhere near us and when he could send a woman to do it for him, but he will think differently when he is actually face to face with us."

"I hope that we don't end up face to face with him at all," Eden said.

"You don't need to be afraid of him, Eden," Pyra said. "We're going back to Earth for Ty and Samira's wedding. We aren't there to see Ryan and we aren't there as part of the university program. He doesn't even have to know that we are back on Earth."

Eden nodded, not wanting to talk about it anymore. The thought lingered in the back of her mind, however, that she doubted they could arrive back on Earth and not have Ryan find out. The task would be to avoid confrontation with him.

Creia stepped up in front of the group and Eden lifted her eyes to the king rather than continuing to dwell on her own thoughts. He held out his arms to all of them and offered a smile that looked softly sad, but also extremely proud.

"Another historic day has arrived," the king said. "As some of our number have returned to the settlement to free the Mikana and begin our journey toward long-awaited reconciliation and building of a new and meaningful cooperation among the species who call our beloved planet home, you will embark on a journey that only one of our kind has made before. You will step on these shuttles and travel off of Uoria and to Earth where you will not only witness the also historic marriage of the first Denynso warrior who has undergone such a ritual, but you will learn more about the planet that we have been working toward creating an alliance with and learning more about. What you learn there will be instrumental in our continued efforts to eradicate the myths and misconceptions that the humans there have of us, and that we have of them so that the lines of communication and cooperation can truly open for the first time in our history. This is a precious and exciting time, and I cannot tell you how proud I am of each one of you. Even though I will be staying behind here with Theia so that we can protect the compound and be waiting in the event that the group from the settlement returns before planned, know that my spirit and my thoughts are with all of you, and that I'll be excited to hear everything that you experienced when you come home."

There was a scattering of applause and Eden realized how nervous everyone around her looked. It was comforting to know that she wasn't the only one who was coping with anxiety related to the trip, but she felt that as one of the few of them who had actually made the trip between the planets it was her responsibility to help soothe and reassure the others who had not ever been off of Uoria, or who had been away from Earth for so long that the thought of returning was almost like going to a foreign planet. She stepped up to Brandy's side and touched a hand to the human woman's back.

The woman turned to look at her and offered a shaky smile.

"It's really happening," Brandy said.

"It is," Eden said, wiggling her newborn son up higher on her shoulder and patting him gently to soothe his soft fussing as he started to awake from his nap. He quieted quickly and she felt his tender belly start to rise and fall slowly with deeper sleep. "Are you excited?"

Brandy looked at the shuttles and then back at her with a sigh.

"I think so. I know it's going to be different. I just hope that I recognize at least some of it."

"You will," Eden reassured her. "It is different, but it's still the same planet. And you'll have us there with you to help you."

Before Brandy could answer, the pilot of each of the shuttles stepped out of the doors of the shuttles and looked out over the group waiting to board.

"All of your cargo is securely packed. The attendants have lists of which passengers should be on which shuttles. Whenever you are ready, you are welcome to come aboard."

The group shifted as they formed a line to approach and climb the steps onto the platform where two attendants stood in the space that connected the two landing bays. They each held notebooks that Eden assumed had lists of the names and other details of the passengers so that they could arrange them into the two shuttles. When she traveled to Uoria from Earth the first time she had been the only one other than the crew who had been aboard. Now both shuttles would be filled to capacity.

Her family approached the first attendant and she checked through her list, then pointed them in the direction of the first shuttle. It looked newer and more complex than the one she had ridden to Uoria the first time. She stepped inside and took a breath of the starkly clean space of the first lounge.

"If you will proceed to your assigned passenger pod room we can begin preparing for takeoff," the attendant said from behind them.

"Will I have my baby with me?" Eden asked, suddenly worrying that they would take Lysander from her and she would be forced to be away from him throughout the journey.

"Yes," the attendant said. "You can keep him in your passenger pod with you. Everyone else, however, must be in individual pods. Please decide if you are going to undergo sedation so that we can begin the process."

The attendant stepped back out of the chamber and

Eden looked around at the people who were gathered in the lounge with her. Zuri, Ero, Elianna, Ciyrs, Ty, Samira, Loralia, and Bannack stood close together in the lounge as if unsure of whether any of them were ready to comply with the instructions from the attendant.

"Are we going to do the sedation?" Bannack asked.

"Did you do it?" Ero asked, looking at Zuri.

"I did on the trip back to Earth the first time," Zuri said.

"What was it like?" Loralia asked.

Zuri shook her head.

"I did it because I didn't want to think about anything on the way," Zuri answered and Eden could see an uncomfortable, guilty look cross Ero's face. "To be honest, though, I didn't like it. It was unnerving to close my eyes and then wake up a few days later. I knew that I was just lying there in my passenger pod, but at the same time, I didn't like knowing that the world was just going on around me and that the crew was awake moving about the shuttle while I was just lying there with no idea what was going on. Now that I know what the flight attendant that was there was actually up to, it makes me even more hesitant to want to be at the mercy of anyone for several days."

Eden nodded.

"Not to mention what happened to Leia."

There was a brief moment of tense silence and then Pyra nodded.

"So we're in agreement. None of us will undergo the sedation. We'll stay awake so that we can stay vigilant about what is going on around us."

"Have you made your decision?" the flight attendant asked as she stepped into the room carrying an armful of blankets.

"Yes," Pyra said. "We don't want to be sedated."

"Very well," she said. "I'll get you situated in your pods and let the captain know that we are prepared for travel."

"How long do we have to wait in the pods until we are able to get out?" Lynx asked.

"Just long enough for the shuttle to get far enough out of the planet's orbit to get into the planned journey path. Should be no more than an hour. When we are traveling safely, the doors to your pod will release and you will be able to get out and move about the shuttle as you please. Refreshments and entertainment will be available then."

Satisfied, Eden and the others followed the attendant into the first passenger pod chamber. As the attendant unlatched the two pods, checked the insides to ensure that they were properly prepared, and draped a blanket across each, Eden turned to Pyra.

"Just an hour," Pyra said, reaching forward and taking Eden's shoulders in his hands.

"I know," she answered.

Pyra pressed a kiss to the top of Lysander's head and then to Eden's lips.

"We'll see everyone in the lounge when we get out," Pyra said to the rest of the group.

They all affirmed and started out of the chamber into the next. Once they were gone, Eden walked over to one of the pods and carefully handed Lysander into Pyra's hands so that he could hold him while she got settled into the pod. This pod was far more comfortable than the seat that she remembered from her first journey, and she felt her nervousness start to dissipate. She settled in and secured her seat belts, positioned her carry-on bag at her feet, then reached for Lysander. Pyra settled the baby into her arms and then draped the blanket over both of them, tucking it in tightly around them.

Eden tilted her face up for one more kiss and then took a deep breath. She looked to the attendant who was standing beside Pyra and nodded.

"I'm ready," she said.

"Just relax," the attendant said. "Enjoy your trip."

Eden smiled and patted Lysander on the back as the large cover of the pod closed over her and clicked into place.

4

———

Leia felt herself shaking with fear as she stared down at the passenger pod. She wished that she and Gyyx were in the same shuttle as the other warriors, the human women, and Loralia, but she wondered if even that would make her feel any less fearful of climbing into that pod.

"It isn't the same shuttle, Leia," Gyyx said comfortingly from behind her, running his hand down her back.

"I know," she said back to him, trying to force her voice above a trembling whisper. "I know it isn't Gyyx, but I can't stop thinking about it."

"Everything is going to be fine this time, Leia. I promise. I'm here."

Leia nodded and took a breath, trying to calm herself. She couldn't help but think about the last time that she was in a shuttle much like this one. Though that shuttle was older, she could just as easily see the image of the interior of it super-imposed over this shuttle. She remembered getting onto the shuttle from Earth headed to Uoria, filled with the excitement of knowing that there was a new adventure waiting for her on the strange and distant planet. She wanted to create art inspired by the planet and the plants and creatures on it, and was dreaming only of the growth that she would experience as an artist on her visit to the planet when she stepped onto the shuttle.

She had never left Earth before and didn't know what to expect from the journey. When the pilot had asked her if she wanted to be put to sleep so that she didn't have to experience the entirety of the five-day journey, she had immediately declined, thinking that it would be so much better to just stay awake and maintain control. She had spent far too much of her life under the influence of men and the substances that they plied her with, and she didn't want to allow herself to spend any more time that way after she had worked so hard to rid herself of this control and shake herself free of the addictions that had defined her for so much of her life.

The pilot had promised her that the takeoff would be the worst part of the journey. He told her that all she had to do was sit in her pod and relax until it released her, and then she could move around the shuttle however she pleased until it was time to land. Though she knew that he thought it was strange that she wanted to stay awake for the full five days rather than just letting it pass easily while she was sleeping, he didn't seem at all concerned about the experience. This flight was going to be no different than any of the other ones that he flew, and he was accustomed to flying on a nearly continuous basis.

What she didn't know when he smiled at her and made his way out of the passenger chamber and into the control room was that it was the final time that she was going to see him. On the second day of her journey the pilot and the attendant who had helped her were slaughtered when the

Klimnu attached their ship to the shuttle and took over. They thought that she was a scientist who could help them with their efforts to take over Uoria. When she told them that she was only an artist who was part of a university exchange programmed designed to allow students from Earth to travel to Uoria and others from Uoria to travel to Earth as well, several of the vile, slimy creatures simply wanted to consider the entire mission aboard the university shuttle a wash and kill her as they had the other two aboard.

The leader of the group, however, hadn't wanted to kill her. Instead, he had taken a strange and disgusting liken to her and decided that he was going to keep her as his own personal pet. She had spent the rest of the trip dangling from a hook hanging from the ceiling of the shuttle. The wounds created in her skin had been so deep that even months later they were still painful and not fully healed.

It had been after this painful, torturous journey, however, that the true torment of the Klimnu had begun. She had no way of knowing then that she was actually the first of the humans who had visited the Denynso compound to encounter the disgusting creatures who were the most hated of the enemies of the warriors. She would later find out that the Denynso didn't even know that she had arrived. The university had lost contact with the shuttle and thought that it had gone off track. They had sent a recovery team to search for the shuttle, hoping that they would simply find that they had gotten lost and needed to be redirected.

Of course they never found them. That was because the ship had gone to Uoria, it had simply landed outside of the barrier of the Denynso compound. Leia didn't remember much of what happened after the shuttle landed. She assumed that the Klimnu had brought her over the boundary and destroyed the shuttle so that no one would find it. Now that she knew more about the planet and the mirrored realm that existed just beneath the ground of the compound, however, she knew better. Even the Denynso didn't know about what was going on under their feet at the time. They didn't know that there had once been an entire colony that had lived there but that then it was used by the Klimnu to hide from the Denynso as they built their defenses.

Leia now assumed that it was through the chambers of that mirrored world that they brought her into the far reaches of the compound and into the dark, dismal prison where she would spend the next 57 days. During the nearly two months of her captivity the KIimnu tortured Leia in ways that left her mind even more scarred than her body, but it was also during that time that they told her information that she would later be able to share with the Denynso that would help them to understand the motivations of the horrific creatures.

She hadn't thought that it would bother her to get back on the shuttle. She hadn't expected that the gruesome memories would flood back to her with the level of intensity that they had as soon as she stepped over the threshold of the lounge and into the passenger chamber. As soon as she had taken that step, however, her bag had slipped from her hand and she felt like she couldn't breathe.

Leia was incredibly thankful that she and Gyyx had been the last of the passengers to take their positions in the shuttle. She didn't feel comfortable enough with the others on the shuttle for them to see her in such paralyzing fear. Gyyx stepped up closer behind her and she could feel his body mold against hers. He was incredibly large, big enough that her head came to rest just beneath his chest and one of his arms was able to fully wrap around her without Gyyx having to reach. It had been this immense size that had immediately attracted and frightened her when she first met the man who had saved her from the coma that she had been in after the Denynso had found her in the prison.

Now it was this size that made her feel safe and protected. She had been completely alone except for the crew of the shuttle the first time that she was on it. There had been no one and nothing to guard her from the Klimnu. This time she was on a full shuttle that held three warriors in addition to her own mate. If something happened, she knew that they would be there and give her more of a chance of getting through the journey unscathed.

"Miss? I'm going to have to ask you to go ahead and get into your pod now," the flight attendant said.

Her voice was calm, but Leia could hear a hint of frustration in it that told her that the woman was eager to get them prepared and off of the ground.

"Do you want them to put you to sleep?" Gyyx asked softly. "It might help if you aren't awake for the next few days."

Leia thought about it for a moment. It was tempting to just lie down and not have to think about anything until they arrived on Earth, but at the same time she didn't relish the idea of giving the Klimnu such power over her, especially now that that iteration of the creatures had been eliminated by the Denynso. She had fought for so long to escape the darkness of her past and prove that she could overcome the torment that she had gone through even before leaving Earth the first time. She didn't want to give up now and resign herself to a life of fear.

She looked up at Gyyx and shook her head.

"No," she told him. "I want to be awake for this."

Leia settled into the pod and focused on Gyyx's face

until the cover came down over her and clicked into place. She closed her eyes and focused on the movement of her breath until she felt the shuttle lurch beneath her and knew that they had taken off. It was truly happening. They had left Uoria and in a matter of days they would be back on Earth.

An hour later she heard the familiar click and hiss of the lid of her pod releasing. It bounced up a few inches and she clambered to release the safety straps holding her against the plush seat and get out of the pod. Gyyx was already standing in the middle of the chamber and she ran into his open arms. He swung her up and held her against his chest, pressing kisses to the side of her neck. When she had first bonded with Gyyx she had hated the way that the massive warrior had picked her up and carried her around like a rag doll. Now, though, she loved to feel the total support and protection of his arms.

Gyyx lowered her to the ground and they walked together toward the long, wide windows that covered the entirety of the far wall of the passenger chamber. The windows of the shuttle she had ridden on her first trip had been smaller, and Leia liked the way that these almost made it seem like there was no window at all, just them floating together through the stars outside.

5

———

"Kyven," Maxim said, grabbing hold of his brother's shoulder and shaking it. "Kyven, get up."

Kyven groaned and gave a half-hearted attempt to roll over away from Maxim's grip, but Maxim held tight to him and gave him a harder shake.

"What?" Kyven moaned, partially opening his eyes.

"You need to get up. Ivy and I need to talk to you."

"What's wrong?" Kyven asked.

His younger brother pulled himself up to sit as he rubbed his eyes. As Maxim watched him his mind flashed to when they were younger. Kyven had woken up in that exact same way since he was just a baby, rubbing his eyes so hard sometimes that their mother had worried he was going to damage his vision. Kyven always said that he was just rubbing the last of his sleep out of them and that he never really felt awake until he had done it enough.

"We just need to talk. Come on. Get up."

Maxim walked out of the bedroom and went back downstairs to where Ivy was waiting in the living room. The house was still quiet in the dawn light and Maxim knew that with the revelry that had occurred the night before it was likely that most of the people in the settlement would be sleeping in for several more hours. Even so, he didn't trust that there weren't ears listening wherever they were in the main portion of the settlement so he knew that he was going to have to bring his brother further out before they could talk.

"What are you going to tell him?" Ivy asked as Maxim sat down on the sofa beside her.

He took her hand from where it rested on her thigh and examined her long, slim fingers.

"Everything. I don't think he even knows as much as I did before we talked to my mother, and now I know so much more. He deserves to know, and he could help us find out everything else."

"What if there is no everything else?" Ivy asked.

Maxim stared at her.

"Please don't start this again, Ivy."

"What do you mean? I am just wondering what if everyone who knows everything is already dead and you are just digging up the past?"

"Sometimes the past is worth digging up. That past is my past, and without that past I don't really have a future. I need to know everything that I can about my father and what caused his death. Him dying changed my life, my brother's life, and my mother's life more than I could ever tell you. I need to know why he died and who caused it. Especially now that I know that it had something to do with the Klimnu and everything that the Klimnu caused on this planet."

He was starting to feel worked up, but Ivy looked at him

with her cool blue eyes and lifted a hand to tenderly stroke the side of his face.

"Alright," she said softly. "I won't ask again. If this matters to you, then it matters to me. I will do whatever I can for you."

Just then, Kyven came down the stairs loudly and walked into the living room still looking like he hadn't managed to rub all of the sleep out of his eyes. He was dressed, but his thick hair hadn't been combed. The wild effect made him look even younger and Maxim felt a surge of protectiveness toward him.

"What did you need to talk to me about?" Kyven asked through a yawn.

"We can't talk here," Maxim said.

He stood up and stalked out of the house, needing to get as far away from the buildings and everyone in them as quickly as he could. He was trying, but he still didn't know who he could trust. He wondered how long it would be until he could truly relax again.

Several minutes later Maxim stopped at the back of the settlement near the wall. It was the place where he had met Ivy and where they had spent many of their early moments together. Here he felt calm and peaceful, and here he knew that there was no one who could get close enough to hear them talking without one of them seeing the person first.

He paced back and forth for several seconds and then looked directly at Kyven.

"Have you ever heard of the Klimnu?" he asked.

"Of course," Kyven said, looking at his brother strangely. "I was right there with you listening to that crazed Denynso ranting about them before he locked us up in the meeting hall."

"I mean before that," Maxim said.

Kyven shook his head.

"No."

"Are you sure? You never heard anyone mention them, even once?"

"I'm sure," Kyven said. "You heard Rey. None of our kind knew that the group that split off went on to become those creatures. Everyone thought that they had just gone out onto the planet on their own and died off."

"Mom knew about them."

Kyven stilled and Maxim saw his eyes widen slightly and then narrow as if he was searching his older brother's face for emotion or explanation.

"What do you mean that Mom knew about them?"

"She knew. She knew that the Klimnu existed and she knew that they came from the group that split off from the rest so long ago."

"Was Rey lying about that, too?"

"No," Maxim said, stepping closer to Kyven. "He doesn't know. According to him, the fate of that group was a complete mystery until we showed up at the settlement and my reaction to the flowers made the Denynso realize that we are the species that transformed into those loathsome creatures."

"I don't understand. How did Mom know? If our leader didn't even know, how could our mother possibly know?"

Maxim took a breath.

"It has to do with the Order." Maxim could see the darkness that rolled over his younger brother's face and he pressed on before Kyven could walk away from him. "When Ivy got me out of the meeting hall we were going to escape to some other part of the planet, but I changed my mind and decided to go back to the kingdom. I thought that it might be safe there. When we got there, we found Athan. He let us into the tunnels."

"We're never supposed to go into the tunnels."

"I know that," Maxim said. "I've spent a lot more time down there than you have. More than I ever wanted to admit to you."

"Why?"

"Because I was curious. I wanted to know what Papa had always talked about when he told us stories about the Order."

"I mean why did you not want to admit it to me?"

Kyven sounded hurt and slightly angry, and Maxim felt a slight pang of guilt.

"You never wanted to know as much as I did," he tried to explain. "You were always satisfied to listen to Mom when she told us that we should stay out of the tunnels and away from anything having to do with the Order. It wasn't enough for me. I needed to know more."

"I don't even understand why Athan would let you down into the tunnels. The Order is gone now. Those tunnels are probably dangerous."

"The Order isn't gone," Maxim told him.

"What?" Kyven asked, sounding shocked at what Maxim had told him.

"The Order isn't gone. It didn't end with Papa dying and it is still going strong."

"Then why aren't we in it?"

"I don't know. That's part of why I wanted to talk to you. Athan was really nervous to let us down in the tunnels, which means that he is still a part of and afraid of the Order. When we were down there we heard two men coming toward us. I couldn't recognize either of their voices, but they almost caught us. We barely made it up through a hatch into one of the hidden entryways before they got to us."

"Does Mom know that the Order still exists?"

Maxim nodded. Kyven seemed to be coming around. The sleepiness was gone from his voice and his eyes, and he was starting to pace slightly back and forth as he listened to Maxim.

"I'm pretty sure that she does," Maxim said. "When we got back home we told her what was going on and she talked about the Order like they are still around. She told me that they knew the entire time what the group had become. They knew about the Klimnu and the horrible things that they did."

"Why didn't they do anything about it?"

"She said that they tried to. She told us that they made alliances with some other species in the badlands and that they tried to fight them off before they left Uoria. It didn't work. By the time that they came back, the generations had forgotten about the Order and even about the Mikana. They only remembered warfare and they destroyed the alliance."

"Who was the other species?"

"She didn't know. That's when she kind of pulled back from us, like she realized what she was talking about and didn't want to do it anymore."

Kyven stared at Maxim for a few long seconds and then suddenly seemed like he had broken out of the spell that his brother had put over him and shook his head.

"What does this have to do with anything, Maxim? So what if the Order still exists? What if they knew about the Klimnu? That is all over now."

"What if it's not?" Ivy asked.

Kyven turned to look at Ivy, the expression on his face like he had forgotten that she was even there.

"What do you mean?" Kyven asked.

"Don't you think that it's strange that every male genera-tion of your family since the beginning of the Order was a member, but neither you or Maxim is?"

Kyven hesitated.

"Our father's dead. Maybe a living relative has to be a part of it when the new people are inducted."

"Mom implied that Papa's death had something to do with the Order and the Klimnu."

"What?"

"When she first told us that the Order knew about the Klimnu, I questioned it and she said 'Why do you think that your father died the way he did?'"

"What did she mean by that?"

"I don't know, but she also said that some members of the Order tried to fight against the Klimnu when they came back after being on Ynn for so long. She said that there was a violent conflict."

"You think that that's when Papa died?"

"I don't know, but I want to. I want to know what happened to him and why the Order tried to cover up the existence of the Klimnu."

"What do you want to do?"

"We need to go talk to Mom again. We need to find out everything that she knows, and then find out everything else that we can."

Kyven looked unsure.

"Maxim, we aren't supposed to know that the Order exists much less anything that they have done or might have done. It is incredibly dangerous for us to even be talking about this. I don't think that we should push it any farther."

"We have to know, Kyven. We have to know why we are the only men in our family who haven't been in the Order.

Papa knew something. Something happened that he knew about and that's why he's dead and why we've been cut off from the Order. We have to know what that was."

"No. You have to know, Maxim. You're the one that this has always mattered to so much. I never cared about the Order or what it meant or when we were going to be a part of it. The only reason I cared when Papa would bring us into the tunnels or show us the secret doors was that we were spending time with him. Now that that's over, I don't think that there could be any benefit in us continuing to dig. We would just be putting ourselves and our mother in serious danger. I just got out of imprisonment because one group wanted to destroy us, I don't need to give another group reason to feel the same way."

"But don't you want to know why the Denynso did that? Don't you want to know what drove Pyra to keep us all captive?"

"He told us. The Klimnu have been the enemies of the Denynso warriors for decades."

"But why? What drove them to that level of cruelty and greed?"

"Maxim, it's over. We're out and the king of the Denynso compound has extended his welcome to us. He wants the conflict to be over, and I think that we should give him that wish. You need to learn to let go."

Kyven turned and started back down toward the settlement. The sun was fully up now and Maxim knew that their privacy would soon be broken as some of the people who had left the celebration earlier got up and started their days. He needed to convince Kyven to join him now or he might lose him again.

"We never got his body back."

Kyven stopped and kept his back to Maxim for a moment before turning to face him.

"What?" he said evenly.

"We never got Papa's body back. Don't you want to know what happened to it? Don't you want to know what could possibly have happened to him that we wouldn't be able to bury him the way he deserved to be buried, and why?"

"It won't change anything, Maxim."

Kyven's voice was softer, almost pleading for Maxim to stop so that he didn't have to think about the painful memories any longer.

"What if it could, though?" Ivy asked, stepping up beside Maxim. He felt her take his hand in hers and he intertwined their fingers familiarly. "So much is happening on Uoria right now, Kyven. The species aren't separate anymore, and they never will be again. Everything that happened here changed that and there's nothing that could happen that will put it back again."

"Everyone is learning more about the planet and how the different settlements and species came to be. People are finally coming together and have the chance of really benefitting each other," Maxim said. "But it isn't over yet. There are things that we don't know, that other people don't even realize that they need to know, and we are the only ones who can really figure it all out. If we don't do it now, if we don't really find out what happened and figure out a way to fix it, Uoria won't ever truly be safe."

"Alright, Maxim," Kyven said, finally sounding resigned to what Maxim had told him. "What do we do?"

6

———

Azra closed his eyes and pressed his hand over them, trying to force his mind to calm down. He was still sitting in his passenger pod even though the top had released and he could hear the voices of the other passengers drifting into the passenger chamber from the lounge where they had gathered. Anyone who looked into the pod right then might have thought that he was afraid of the trip, or that he was feeling sick because of the unusual, unknown movements of the shuttle. What they couldn't know is that the trip didn't bother him at all. Unlike some of the others who had climbed aboard the shuttle for their first venture off of Uoria, he was excited about the adventure and had absolutely no anxiety about the unknown that awaited them. The feelings that he was dealing with were something far more unexpected, and far more frightening, than any space travel could be.

The door to his pod opened and Azra took his hand away from his eyes to look up at who opened it. Elise, the beautiful flight attendant who he had first seen standing on the platform directing passengers into the shuttle, stood over the pod, smiling down into his face.

"Azra?" she said brightly. "Are you alright?"

Azra forced a smile and nodded.

"I'm fine," he said.

"All of the other passengers are out in the lounge and I was getting ready to serve breakfast if you'd like to join them."

Azra nodded again but didn't move.

"Thank you," he said. "Maybe I'll join them in a minute."

Elise looked at him strangely.

"Are you feeling alright?" she asked. "Have you rethought about being put into sleep so that you don't have to actually experience the flight? If you have, that's alright. It can still be done."

"No, no," Azra said, waving his hands as if trying to convince her that, that was not the case. In fact, the last thing he wanted was to sleep through the entire time that he had on the shuttle, and with Elise. "I'm going to be fine. I guess I'm just getting used to the whole idea of space travel."

The smile returned to Elise's plush red lips and she pushed the lid of his pod completely open.

"Come on. You'll feel much better once you have something to eat."

Azra released the safety straps that held him to the seat inside the pod and climbed out, carefully pulling his blanket along with him and wrapping it around himself before turning around to face Elise. She laughed slightly.

"Chilly?" she asked.

"A little bit. I'm not used to being inside places like this."

"I can ask the captain if he can increase the temperature in your pod a little if you would like."

"No, that's alright," Azra answered quickly. "I don't really plan on spending much time in there, and if I am, I'll have my blanket. No reason to go to any trouble for me."

Elise smiled again and started toward the lounge. Azra followed behind her, trying as hard as he could to keep his eyes from only focusing on the sway of her hips and the deep curve of her waist. When they got into the lounge Elise disappeared into a crew area and Azra crossed the room to where Gyyx sat at one of the tables against the window. He was eating what looked like small nuts out of a bowl and he looked up at Azra with a confused expression when he approached.

"Are you going for some sort of fashion statement with that?" Gyyx asked, taking the shell of one of the nuts out of his mouth and tossing it into a cup beside him.

"No, I am not going for a fashion statement," Azra replied, the aggravation evident in his voice. "I'm trying to be...subtle."

"Subtle?" Gyyx asked. "What the hell could you be subtle about wrapped up in a blanket like....oh, damn." Azra nodded at him. "Who is she?"

"The attendant, Elise," Azra said.

Gyyx chuckled and took another shell from his mouth.

"Well, she's a good one, at least you've got that."

Azra felt his hands clench and his jaw tighten almost painfully with a surge of defensive anger that flowed through him at Gyyx's words.

"What do you mean by that?" he snarled.

"Calm down, Azra," Gyyx said. "My mate is standing about twelve feet from you. There's nothing for you to be so defensive about."

Azra tried to calm down, but he couldn't seem to control the waves of emotion that were moving through him at unnerving speed.

"Don't talk to me like that, Gyyx."

"What's going on over here?" Reston asked, crossing the lounge to stand beside the table.

"Why don't you tell him, Azra?"

"I want to kill him," Azra growled.

It was the most overwhelming blend of emotions that he had ever experienced. The intensity of his aggression toward Gyyx was blinding, even though in the logical part of his mind he knew that the fellow warrior posed no threat to Elise. Combined with the fierce arousal that seemed to be getting more and more evident by the moment, these violent emotions only further confirmed what he had realized only moments after seeing Elise for the first time. She was meant to be his mate.

"Why is that?" Reston asked.

"I mentioned that Elise seemed like a good woman," Gyyx answered.

He was continuing to work his way through the bowl of nuts and something about his incessant crunching and tossing of the shells into the cup beside him only made Azra's feelings of aggression toward him increase.

"The flight attendant?" Reston asked.

"Yes," Azra said through gritted teeth.

"Damnit," Reston said. "You are seriously going to leave me as one of the last maybe six warriors without mates, aren't you?"

"Just make sure that you are being careful, Azra," Gyyx said, his tone suddenly serious as the teasing disappeared.

"What do you mean?" Azra asked.

"Be sure that you are completely positive about this woman before you do anything with her."

"What are you saying, Gyyx?"

The other warrior sighed and looked into Azra's eyes intently.

"Look, Elise seems like a really nice girl. She's sweet and she's pretty, but so was the flight attendant who helped Ullie betray us to the Klimnu. I just want you to know what you're doing."

Azra made an adjustment so that the surging erection that he'd had since climbing aboard the shuttle wouldn't be as obvious and walked away from the table. He didn't want to listen to any more of this. He had been part of plenty of good-natured ribbing when the other warriors had mated, but now that he was going through the almost painful signs that he was close by his intended mate, it no longer seemed like something that they should be laughing about. This wasn't a Denynso woman or even a human woman who had come to the compound with the intention of staying for a while. This was a flight attendant who he would have only a matter of a few days with and the thought that she was meant to his mate sent a sinking feeling through his gut.

Holding the balled-up blanket in one hand, Azra stalked through the lounge and back into the passenger chamber. He dropped into his pod and let his head fall back against the seat.

"I guess that being in the lounge didn't agree with you as much as I thought that it would."

Azra looked up and saw Elise standing beside him again. She was carrying a tray balanced on one hand and a folded stand in the other. In one swift movement she propped the stand up and rested the tray on it.

"That was pretty impressive," Azra said.

Elise laughed and nodded.

"I've gotten a lot of practice," she said. "You don't want to know how many of these trays I've managed to splatter across the floor, or even worse, on a few passengers."

"I want to know everything about you."

The words came out of Azra's mouth before he was able to control them and he wished that he could gather them up and push them out of the way before she heard them, but the softly startled look in her eyes told him that Elise had heard. She opened her mouth slightly and then closed it again. Azra didn't know what to say to her, but started to apologize. Before he could, she looked down at the tray and spoke again.

"I made this for you," she said. "It isn't exactly what was on the menu for breakfast, but it's what I ate on my very first trip. I was really nervous and something about this made me feel better. I don't know if it was actually the food or not, but I've eaten it every first breakfast on every trip since and it keeps me calm for the rest of the trip."

Azra felt his heart swell slightly and he gave her a small smile.

"Thank you."

She nodded and walked away. After a few steps she stopped, turned back around to him like she was going to say something, and then turned sharply back around and left the chamber, closing the sliding door behind her. Once she was gone, Azra slid forward in his seat and looked at the plate on the tray in front of him. He didn't recognize most of the food, but the smell was delicious and he realized in that moment how hungry he was. Taking a swig first of the hot, rich drink in a mug beside the plate, he dug into the food, savoring every bite and wondering if it tasted so incredibly delicious because the food itself was so good, or because he could imagine the delicate, pale hands of his intended mate carefully crafting it for him.

7

"So what do we do now?" Kyven asked.

He was pacing back and forth in front of Maxim and Ivy in large swathes now, taking longer steps the faster the thoughts in his mind spun. Everything seemed to be coming at him too quickly and he didn't know how he was supposed to process it all. This was the first time that he had left the kingdom, just as it was with Maxim, but Maxim was older than he was and had a confidence and sense of calm that exceeded even the extra years that he had on his brother. Maxim was the one who would be able to handle all of this. Not him. Not Kyven. He had always been perfectly fine with being the younger brother and living somewhat in Maxim's shadow. At least living in Maxim's shadow enabled him to escape the expectation that he would live in his father's, or grandfather's, or great-grand-fathers.

The truth was that Kyven had listened to the stories that their father had told them more with a sense of fear and dread than one of excitement like Maxim. He wouldn't consider himself cowardly and it wasn't that he didn't want to do anything, it was simply that the thought of being a part of the Order and the mysterious activities they were involved in wasn't something that appealed to him. The thoughts that Maxim and Ivy had conjured of his father, however, had made Kyven realize that his connection with the Order was far from being over. He owed it to the memory of his father to find out really what happened and ensure that it never happened again.

"We have to go back and talk to Mom again," Maxim said.

Kyven shook his head.

"No."

"Why not?"

"She isn't going to tell us anything, Maxim. She is going to be too afraid. She already told you far too much and she's not going to be willing to put herself at any more risk."

"But she told me in the first place," Maxim said. "That means that the hold that the Order had on her is starting to fade. Remember when we were younger. She would never even mention the Order. I don't honestly think that I heard her say those specific words until Ivy and I were there talking to her last."

"She always just spoke after Papa or made references that she hoped we would understand," Kyven said.

"Exactly. But when we were talking to her, she said it. She said it right out loud. She is probably still afraid, but that fear is letting up. We're adults now, Kyven. She doesn't have to hide things from us anymore."

"Of course she does. It doesn't matter how old we get, we are always going to be her only children. She has never wanted us to know about the Order. Why would she start now?"

"I didn't say that she wanted us to know," Maxim said. "I

just said that the fear that she has had for so long is starting to lessen and the control that the Order has always had on her is starting to go away. That means that she is going to be more willing to tell us what we need to know."

"And what if she doesn't? What if she just shuts down and won't tell us anything?"

"She loved Papa more than anything in the world, Kyven. Losing him absolutely destroyed her, and you know it. You remember what it was like when she had to tell us that he was dead. It was like it ripped her heart out and she was never really the same."

"I don't think that she believes the story that they told her about how he died," Ivy said.

Kyven looked at the small blond woman and cocked his head slightly. She was difficult to figure out. She was quiet much of the time and didn't seem to mind disappearing into the background when he and Maxim were talking, but in the next moment she would interject herself in a way that was bold and almost unnerving. Coming from a family that revolved around secrets, it felt strange when a new face arrived who was so intertwined with everything even though he barely knew her.

"Why would you say that?" Kyven asked.

"There was something about the way that she said it to Maxim. There was a catch in her voice when she said 'Why do you think that your father died the way that he did.' It was like she was having to convince herself of something in her mind. What did she tell you about how he died?"

"We've already talked about this," Maxim said, stepping closer to Ivy and looking at her strangely as if she had forgotten a conversation that they had. "Remember? When we were on the way here from the compound I told you everything about that night."

"I know," Ivy said, looking at Maxim. She paused briefly and then looked back at Kyven. "I want to know what he remembers."

"Why?" Kyven asked. "If Maxim already told you about that night, why do you need to have it rehashed again?"

"What you remember about that night and what your mother told you and what Maxim remembers might be very different. If we compare the two, we might be able to learn more just from that."

"She's right," Maxim said. "You were younger, but I'm sure that you remember that night. Tell us what you remember."

Kyven sighed. He didn't want to have this conversation. He didn't want to think through that horror again.

"I remember Athan coming to the door. Papa had been gone for so long, and for a minute I thought that it might be him knocking on the door trying to be funny. I was in the kitchen when Mom opened the door and when I looked around the corner I could see Athan standing in the living room with her. He looked like he had been dragged through hell and back. His clothes were tattered and there was dried blood on his skin. I remember hoping that Papa didn't look that bad and wondering if Mom had enough of the herbs that he liked in his baths when he usually came home from those missions. I knew where the herbs grew and I could go get them for her if she didn't have enough to put in the water for when he came inside."

"So that's why you were putting on your shoes that night when Mom came in the room and told us that she had to talk to us," Maxim said.

Kyven nodded.

"I was lacing my shoes when I heard Mom make a sound like she was choking. I looked into the living room and she was standing there with her hand on her chest, pressing down as if she were trying to hold her heart in place. I guess in a way she was. I was so wrapped up in listening to what Athan was saying to her that I completely forgot to tie my shoe. I just sat there holding the laces."

"You could hear them talking?" Maxim asked.

He sounded surprised by the revelation and Kyven realized that Ivy might be right. He could know more about that night than Maxim did, and it could make a difference.

"Yes," Kyven said. "I was listening to them before you even came into the room."

"I couldn't hear them at all. I just saw them talking. I just thought that he only told her what she told us."

"You were so young," Ivy said. "She probably told you what she thought that you could handle. She was trying to protect you."

"What did Athan say to her?" Maxim asked, seeming to ignore the attempted comfort by his partner.

Kyven let his mind wander back to that night. He could still see Athan standing in the living room, part of his body obscured by his mother standing in between them. She was drying one of the dishes from dinner with a white towel and he remembered thinking that everything about her at that moment, the moment before their world shattered, seemed so peaceful and calm.

"He told her that Papa was dead. She asked him what happened, and at first he didn't want to say anything else. I didn't have any idea why, but he seemed scared, like he thought that there was someone who would hear anything that he said and that it could cause serious problems. Mom pulled him further into the room and turned so that her back was to the door and Athan was facing it. I guess she thought that that would help keep his voice from traveling through the door just in case someone was standing right outside. She asked him again what happened and he just looked at her and said 'They found out, Ellora. He knew what was happening and he couldn't fight it anymore.'"

"Was 'they' the Order?" Maxim asked.

"Or the Klimnu?" Ivy asked.

Kyven looked up at her again and saw that she was staring at Maxim.

"Remember what we talked about when we were on our way from the compound? Your mother said that your father died because of the Order and the Klimnu, but she didn't say which one was the one that was actually responsible for his death. He could have been evolved into Klimnu and been eliminated by the Order because they were fighting against the Klimnu and seeking vengeance for that group destroying their allies."

"But it also could be that he knew too much about the Klimnu because the Order was changing and he wasn't," Maxim said.

"Athan knows what happened," Kyven said. "He knows why Papa died and what happened to him."

Suddenly Kyven was feeling less distant from the situation. He could remember that night so powerfully. He could see the look in Athan's eyes, and hear the tremble in his mother's voice. Everything changed that night. He hadn't really made the connection before, but the kingdom became tenser after that. There was a sense of guarded distrust and the hint of danger that seemed to underscore everything that anyone in the kingdom did, especially his mother. She had started to disappear for lengths of time and her insistence that they not talk about the Order became even more aggressive. It was like she was trying to eliminate them in her children because they haunted her so much already in her heart.

"How long will it take you to get ready to leave?" Maxim asked.

"I only need to pack the few things that I brought with me."

"We need to make sure that we have enough supplies to get us through the journey," Maxim said. "We'll leave this afternoon," he said. "We're going home."

8

Azra leaned against the wall of the observation dome staring out into the endless blanket of stars that stretched around the shuttle. It was deep in the night, not that he would have noticed any difference had it been in the middle of the day. They were too far from either planet for either sun to impact how the sky looked. Instead, he was surrounded by continuous, almost tangible blackness and stars.

He didn't know how long he had been standing there, unable to sleep as all the others were doing, when he suddenly felt the presence of someone else step into the observation dome with him. Azra turned and saw Elise standing in the doorway timidly like she was unsure if she should enter or not. He noticed that she was no longer wearing the prim flight attendant's uniform that she was always wearing when she was interacting with them in the pods or the lounge during the day. Instead, she was wearing a long, flowing white gown with wide sleeves that closed tightly at the wrists. Hair that was usually pinned up and away from her neck and face tumbled down around her shoulders and a strand that fell in front showed that it stretched down to her waist.

She was even more breathtakingly beautiful than he already knew and he felt his stomach clench as his uncontrollable desire for her reached a new peak.

"Am I bothering you?" she finally asked softly.

"Of course not," he said, gesturing for her to come closer. "Please, join me."

Elise stepped inside and came to Azra's side. He breathed in the full, sweet smell of her and felt his mind go slightly dizzy.

"Is it true that you've never left your planet?" she asked after they stared together into the stars for a few moments.

Azra nodded.

"It is," he said. "Only one of the Denynso have left Uoria, and that was an emergency."

"An emergency?" she asked, sounding worried.

"His mate is from Earth. He offended her horribly within the first 24 hours of her being on Uoria and she promptly got back on the shuttle that hadn't left yet and went back to Earth. He knew that he couldn't live without her, so the king called for another shuttle and he met her there."

Elise laughed.

"I guess a man will do anything when he realizes that he has done something wrong to the woman he loves."

"Yes," Azra said.

The heat that was building between them was increasing and he felt his erection pressing almost painfully against the front of his pants. If the aggression and violence that he was feeling toward his friends didn't tell him what he already knew about Elise, his arousal did. It was perhaps the most potent and disruptive of the signs that a Denynso man was near the woman who was intended to be his mate and lifelong partner.

"How did he know that she was going to take him back?"

"She is the only person who he will ever love. She is human so had no way of knowing for sure that she felt the same attachment to him that he has for her, but he really had no other option but to go after her. If he didn't, he would be alone and wondering about her for the rest of his life."

"How did he know that she was the only one for him?"

"How much do you know about the Denynso?" Azra asked.

"Not much," she admitted. "I've heard of impossibly large, gorgeous men born to fight and who mate for life."

Azra gave a short laugh at the description and nodded.

"I can attest for the 'born to fight' and 'mate for life' elements of that," he said.

"I can attest to the others," Elise said softly, her eyes drinking in Azra standing in front of her in only loose sleeping pants.

Azra glanced away and then back at her, his heart pounding in his chest.

"Elise, I-" he started, but she cut him off before he could say any more.

"How does a Denynso man know that he has found the woman who is meant to be his mate?" she asked.

Her voice was low and sultry, making her seem innocent and incredibly sexy at the same time.

"He can feel it," Azra answered. "He gets aggressive and defensive, even more so than usual, as he prepares to protect his mate and their future children. He will lash out against anyone but her. This frequently causes issues among the warriors, but fortunately so many of them are already mated that they understand what's going on and are more willing to help the warrior who is in that phase get through it rather than fight back."

"What else?" she asked.

"His eyes start to change. They will shift from the color that he was born with to orange and back again up until he is fully mated to her."

Elise looked up into his eyes and Azra knew that she could see these changes happening as he stared back at her. She stepped closer to him and he felt his breath catch. She was only a few inches away now and his body ached for her. He could barely control himself and he looked away into the stars again for a few moments to quiet his thoughts.

"What else?" she asked.

Azra looked back at her and the tip of her tongue slipped out to run across her bottom lip just briefly. He reached down and took her hand, bringing it up to flatten it against his bare chest.

"His skin gets hot to the touch. Eventually it will get so hot that any other woman around him will not be able to stand being close to him because the heat actually radiates off of his body, forcing them back."

"It is only that hot to other women?" she asked.

"Yes," he answered, applying gentle pressure to her hand so that she stroked his chest. "His mate will only notice that it is warm."

She made a soft, appreciative sound and nodded lightly.

"Is there anything else that tells a Denynso warrior that he has found his mate?" she asked.

Azra could barely breathe for the intensity of the need for her that was pulsating through him. He wanted to control it, but he knew that he couldn't deny what was happening deep within him. He wanted her like he had never wanted anything, like he didn't think was possible to want someone, and he couldn't resist that need any longer.

"His body tells him," he said quietly.

"How?" Elise asked.

"He becomes hungry for her," Azra said, "Needing her in a way that is completely overwhelming, and it won't go away until he finally mates with her."

"Are you hungry?" Elise whispered.

Azra took her hand again and led it down his body, not breaking the connection between their eyes, until it reached the front of his pants. He turned her hand carefully and pressed on it to cup it around the hard swell that continued to push toward her. She gasped slightly and he felt a surge of strength within him. Elise stepped forward to completely close the space between them and touched a kiss to his chest, running her parted lips across his skin and occasionally allowing the tip of her tongue to follow the path. He groaned, touching her hair softly as she continued the attention along his body.

"Elise," he said, trying to control his voice. "If this is happening too fast for you..."

His mind was spinning. He didn't want to think about what Gyyx had said. He wanted only to listen to what his mind and body were telling him, and that was that Elise was meant to be his mate.

"I know what I'm doing, Azra," she said. "I've known from the moment I saw you."

At that, Azra reached forward and swept Elise into his arms, lifting her up his body so that he could capture her mouth with his. Her legs wrapped around his hips and she welcomed the kiss, parting her lips under the insistence of his tongue so that he could explore her fully. Azra held her close to his body and lowered himself to his knees, supporting her and protecting the back of her head as he carefully lay her back on the floor. He would have wanted to be in a bed with her, but the closest thing that he had was his pod and that was in a room he was sharing with Jonathan. The best he could do was lay her beneath the stars and bond with her surrounded by the most spectacular beauty that he had ever witnessed.

Azra used one hand to release the ties at the front of his sleep pants and then kicked them off. Just that quickly he was completely bare, but she was still covered from her neck to her ankles. The soft fabric of her gown against his skin was enticing, and he spent a moment resting on top of her, kissing her languidly. Finally he felt her reach down and take hold of either side of her skirt. She gathered it in her fingers so that it crept up her legs, gradually causing more and more of their skin to touch. With each new inch Azra felt like his control was disappearing.

Finally Elise lifted her hips slightly and pulled the gown out from under her so that it pooled around her waist. This movement revealed that she had worn nothing beneath the gown and Azra couldn't hold back any longer. Gently pressing her thighs apart with one hand, Azra positioned his hips between them and let the tip of his erection slide along the warm wetness of her core. Elise moaned and arched slightly, but Azra didn't delve into her quite yet. As much as he wanted her, he also wanted this incredible moment to last as long as possible.

Wrapping his hand around the base of his cock, Azra used the tip to stroke Elise's folds, focusing on her sensitive pearl until she was nearly sobbing. At last he released his grip and allowed the tip of his erection to slide down to nestle just at her opening. Elise parted her legs slightly further and pressed forward with her hips, accepting him as he eased into her. She felt incredibly tight and hot, embracing him intimately as he sank further into her.

Azra sat back on his knees and pulled her hips forward so that they balanced on his lap. As he drove himself deeply into her, encouraging her to open to him, Elise took hold of the hem of her gown and slid it off over her head. Azra let one of his hands cup a full breast, massaging it tenderly. After a few moments he tipped forward so that he was hovering over her again and slightly increased his speed and intensity. Each stroke drew a whimper of pleasure from Elise's chest and she reached up to wrap her arms around Azra's shoulders. The incredible sensations created by her body were building up inside Azra intensely and when he leaned down to take one taut pink nipple into his mouth, her cry made him lose control. In a few final thrusts he toppled into a blinding climax and had to bite down into her shoulder to prevent himself from roaring in pleasure.

Elise's body began to spasm around him, each tiny pulse meeting his throbs and milking him as he spilled into her. She was trembling in his arms, her head tucked into the curve of his shoulder and neck so that she could kiss along his collarbone as she tried to regain control of her breath. As his body cooled and relaxed, an incredible warmth flowed through him. He felt more content and at peace than he ever had, and in that moment it felt like her heartbeat against his chest was beating for both of them.

TBC

(To be continued in book V...)